Paranoid

by

Bo Turner

Sarah,
Happy Birthday!
be careful in Italy!

Bo.

DORRANCE PUBLISHING CO., INC.
PITTSBURGH, PENNSYLVANIA 15222

This is a work of fiction. Names, characters, places, and incidents are either the product of the author's imagination or are used fictitiously, and any resemblance to actual persons, living or dead; events; or locales is entirely coincidental.

ISBN: 978-1-4349-0940-4
eISBN: 978-1-4349-5782-5
Printed in the United States of America

First Printing

For more information or to order additional books, please contact:
Dorrance Publishing Co., Inc.
701 Smithfield Street
Pittsburgh, Pennsylvania 15222
U.S.A.
1-800-788-7654
www.dorrancebookstore.com

To Bud Hill, for showing me I can write;
To Ed Barber, for giving me the chance to write;
And to Ron Dupont, for helping me learn to write.

Chapter One

Jeff Murdock had made a complete conversion. Or so he thought. He did not think one newspaper story could change his life so drastically.

Jeff woke up that brisk morning in March of 2007 and, as usual, did his morning prayer. He usually just did the Morning Prayer part of the Liturgy of the Hours, but sometimes included the Office of Readings. These are the rote prayers used by the clergy and avowed religious in the Catholic Church to help them maintain a spiritual life. It would oftentimes give him solace or inspiration. He poured himself and his wife, Jennifer, each a cup of coffee. He knew she wasn't getting up yet, but she liked having her coffee sitting ready for her, and he liked doing those little acts of affection for her. In their thirty years of marriage, he'd only been able to do it since the kids moved out on their own, but he felt like he was "spoiling her," and he liked it. In his mind, little acts like that made up for all the time he ignored her. He got dressed and went to work.

Jeff was a salesman. He had been working for Plumbco Plumbing Supply for about fifteen years. As the company grew, it was bought by larger and larger conglomerates. Along the way, Jeff had been made sales manager, and then vice president of sales. But he still saw himself as a salesman. He enjoyed arriving for work early each day—even before his secretary, Mary—and starting a pot of coffee. He would then sit and read his newspaper. Howard was usually there. Howard worked the counter, the center for inside sales where plumbers would come in and buy what they needed for the day's work. This part of the operation had a higher profit margin than the area in which Jeff focused, but he and Howard both knew that it was the volume of sales which Jeff generated—by selling to big jobs and to those shops that maintained an inventory—that made Plumbco what it is.

Howard had been with Plumbco for a long time. He had a great knowledge of plumbing supplies and a vast amount of institutional knowledge related to Plumbco. Howard was, however, never going to be an outside salesman, and he knew it. While Jeff and Howard got along quite well, Howard had trouble relating to people. He seemed agitated around strangers and was uncomfortable in new surroundings. If he did not know a person, his answers to questions were brief and abrupt. He, in turn, would ask questions that seemed unrelated and sometimes inappropriate. And then, there was his appearance. Howard was short and stocky. He always seemed to have sores and scabs on his arms that he attributed to mishaps in the warehouse. The fact is, the open sores and scabs came from an obsessive behavior in which

Howard would pick, scratch, and squeeze the most benign of flaws he saw on his arms.

Usually, Mary would come in early as well, but always after the coffee was ready. Jeff would bring her a cup, and they would talk for several minutes. Mary was about fifteen years younger than Jeff, and very pretty. She found him good company in the mornings. She was fond of Jeff, but not in a sexual way. She thought he was attractive, but she really just liked his company. The fact that he never made reference to her looks and recognized her for her ability made him even more attractive to her, but a workplace affair was out of the question for her.

Mary's high school sweetheart proposed to her a year and a half after she graduated. He was a couple of years older, and he had been on his own for a while. They had dated for more than three years, and it was what Mary expected. After the wedding, Mary soon found out what Jim was really like. He constantly wanted to have sex. At first, Mary was more than happy to oblige. Soon, however, she began to feel more like an object than a partner. They never made love; they just had sex. When Mary did not want to "do it," Jim would badger her unceasingly until she gave in. Inevitably, Mary got pregnant and gave birth to a beautiful little girl. Jim continued with his badgering; only now, that was the only time he wanted to be around Mary. He drank more, went out with his friends, played softball (where he drank even more), and would return home drunk just to score with his sure thing.

Eventually, Mary had enough. She packed up her stuff and some things for the baby, and returned home to her mother.

While Mary liked the attention—and the respect—Jeff showed her, she convinced herself it was best to never have a relationship with a man again. She dated occasionally, but never anything serious. Men were, after all, all the same.

"Man, we've got a truckload of stuff going out today," Howard said. "A lot of pipe. I hope we don't run out of pipe before our next load gets here."

"We won't," Jeff said. "There's a truck coming in from Ocala this afternoon. They're going to loan us some."

As Plumbco grew, it now had fifty branches in Florida, Georgia, and Alabama. The branches in Gainesville—where Jeff worked—Lake City, Jacksonville, and Ocala often worked together, helping each other with inventory.

Jeff got his coffee, picked up his newspaper, and went to his office. He stopped on Page 1A. He could not believe what he was reading.

Roger, the general manager of the branch—sort of the vice president of operations—was walking by and said, "Good morning," through the open door. Jeff looked different, different enough for Roger to stop and ask, "Is everything okay?"

"Yeah," Jeff said. "I'm okay."

He continued reading, unable to fully grasp what he was reading.

It was a story in the local paper telling how the *New York Times* petitioned for the release of the "Family Jewels" under the Freedom of Information Act. The *Times*, of course, was receiving resistance. Roger came into Jeff's office and began reading over his shoulder.

Roger was a country boy and a perfectionist. The latter character trait was one reason he had done so well with Plumbco. But, it was also the reason his future was so limited.

Roger knew company policy—all company policies. He stuck to the letter of the law and never took a risk: not in personnel, not in credit procedures, not in inventory or purchasing, not in anything. As a result, Roger's branch never lost money. It rarely got stuck by a plumber going out of business and never lost money on a big job because of the assurances he required. But, his branch also rarely showed a great deal of profit in dollars earned. In profit percentage, Roger had had a few good years, but overall, nothing outstanding.

Also, Roger was a perfectionist to such an extent that he often drove good employees away. There was the legend of the one evening, after discovering that one pallet rack was four inches out of line with all other pallet racks, Roger had all salaried men and two hourly employees stay late, unload each section of the rack, move it forward four inches, reload it, and go to the next section. Each section was twelve feet long, and the row was sixty feet long. The mission took six men, not counting Roger, the supervisor, two and a half hours.

"I ain't no spy," Roger said about the article, "but that seems kind of stupid to me."

"I…I don't understand it, either," Jeff said. "Why would they do such a thing?"

"You know how government works: in order to get more money, show how much you do."

"Yeah," Jeff said. "But I don't think anybody really knows what the CIA (Central Intelligence Agency) does. Why would they keep such a record?"

Chapter Two

In the 1960s, the CIA was caught in the embarrassment of the Bay of Pigs operation in Cuba. In the 1970s, it was the apparent CIA involvement in the Watergate scandal and countless other operations "sanctioned" by the CIA, but not a part of its official operation performed by independent contractors that included domestic operations involving spying on Americans. Director of the CIA James Schlessinger, as he was leaving his post to become secretary of state, ordered that all operations be recorded and detailed. When William Colby took over as director, he locked the files away. He was convinced that it was necessary to undertake operations that were strictly prohibited by law. For those operations, it was okay, Schlessinger thought, even wise, to hire people outside of the company. These operatives would not be restricted by company policy. Heck, if they broke the law, it would not be the problem of the CIA. It would be their problem.

But what few people within the company knew, and none of the operatives knew, was that Director Schlessinger would assign agents the task of keeping detailed records of all their dirty tricks and illegal activities. Of course, for matters of national security, this report would remain classified. But it would include many, many details of the operations that had goals in line with the company's goals, but not be a part of CIA operations. When Gerald Ford became president, Henry Kissinger reviewed the 700-page document and gave President Ford a five-paged synopsis. It told of how the CIA had indeed spied on Americans involved in the anti-war movement, wiretapped reporters, and placed them under surveillance. While Kissinger told Ford that many of the CIA's operations were "clearly illegal," he did not tell Ford of some of the worst revelations. The document, Kissinger said, raised some "profound moral questions."

These records were somewhat jokingly given the name the "Family Jewels." Everyone knew that, should these documents fall into the hands of unpatriotic people or the press, they would have the CIA by the balls. The document kept the name Family Jewels, but Kissinger called it "The Horror's Book."

Now, the *New York Times* knew it existed. They knew it had been "declassified." And, they wanted to see it. The *Times* filed a Freedom of Information Act request in January of 2007. This was, as one might expect, not a request the CIA was looking forward to fulfilling. The official response was a concern for national security, but they were now asking themselves, "Why the hell did we keep these records?"

Chapter Three

Roger was a good manager, a decent boss, but he could be clueless. Although Roger was a meticulous record keeper, he could see how insane it was for any operation—government or private industry—to do things it knew was wrong and then keep records of everything they did wrong. Jeff had to get out of there. He called Jennifer.

"Hey, any chance you can grab an early lunch?"

"I don't know, hon. We're kind of busy today." Jennifer was a nurse practitioner at a local nursing home. Since a doctor was not always in the building, she was often left to manage the daily healthcare needs of the residents. When one resident had problems, several tended to have the same problem. It was often hard to tell if it was psychosomatic or an outbreak.

Jennifer worked hard to become a nurse practitioner. She became pregnant while she was working on her RN (Registered Nurse) degree at the community college in South Florida. Her instructors did not expect Jennifer to complete the program. She did, despite bouts of morning sickness.

When she and Jeff moved to North Florida, she began working on her BSN at the University of Florida (UF)—one class per semester. Again, her professor did not think she could do it. Finally, when she began work on her master's degree at UF, it was a long process. In fact, the university changed its policy so that there is now a time limit on how long it takes to finish a master's degree. Jennifer felt sure it was the long duration of her master's work that inspired the college to change its policy.

During that time, Jennifer gave birth to two children. She focused on her children and her studies. Jeff poured himself into his work, putting in sometimes sixty to seventy-hour weeks. Jeff seemed a little more relaxed since the kids moved out, but Jennifer now knew that they had nothing in common.

"What's wrong? You sound a little shaken."

"I just read something in the paper today that's got me a little worried. We can talk later."

"If it's really important, I'll get a way," she said.

"No, it'll be okay," Jeff said half-heartedly. "I am probably overreacting. I'll see you at home. I love you."

"Love you, too."

Usually, if Jeff and Jennifer said they would talk about something later, they never did. Sometimes, they both just forgot—the matter was not that important. Other times, one or the other sat quietly, letting the subject gnaw at his or her gut, but not wanting to broach the subject. That's what usually led to fights. Each thought if they were quiet long enough, it would go away. Unresolved issues were preferred to fighting.

As Jennifer passed the nurses' station, she saw a newspaper laying there. *There's a chance we might talk*, she thought. After asking, she took the paper, folded it over, and stuck it in the pocket of her lab coat. She would read it later.

Chapter Four

Jeff recalled when Jim Stewart first approached him. Jeff had been both a good student and a great athlete in high school. Starting in his junior year, Jeff was recruited by a few different colleges to play football, but it came down to two: West Point and Columbia. It was a foregone conclusion by several that Jeff would choose West Point. His father hoped Jeff would, because it would be much easier on him financially. Even though Columbia offered to pay his tuition and books, and give Jeff a job to cover his housing costs, Bill Murdock knew that there were other costs involved in going to college, and the Army would cover those costs if Jeff chose West Point. Jeff had even received the letter of appointment from a local congressman—an avid football fan.

When Jim Stewart visited Jeff's Catholic high school campus on recruiting day, he was very interested in Jeff. Jim went to high school and college campuses recruiting people—the best and the brightest—for jobs in the federal government. That day, he was representing the FBI (Federal Bureau of Investigation). But Jim later learned that West Point had laid claim to Jeff. Jim believed the FBI did not want to compete with the military.

Special Agent Jim Stewart was very much a team player. He was in the ROTC (Reserve Officers' Training Corps) program at Liguori University and an officer in the United States Army. After his hitch was over, Stewart applied at the FBI, the place where he had intended to end up. He had been a field agent for only a few years when the Bureau wanted to transfer Stewart to recruiting. He was not truly excited about the move. Jim thought perhaps it was a statement about his performance as a field agent. After being assured it was not, Jim accepted the assignment and, as always, did his best.

"That's okay," Jim said to Jeff. "Chances are, you'll end up at Justice, one way or the other."

Jeff did not really know what the recruiter meant. He tossed his head and threw his long black hair over his broad shoulders. "Okay," he said. "I guess I'll see you around."

Jeff disappointed a lot of people when he chose to go to Columbia instead of West Point. A year and a half later, after Jeff quit Columbia following his sophomore season, he was sitting at his parents' house, trying to plan out his life. Even though two of the six kids in his family had moved out, Jeff felt crowded living in that house. His father, a big man who believed in stern discipline, strode in.

"Jeff, telephone."

"Hello, Jeff. This is Jim Stewart," the voice on the other end said.

"Who?"

"Special Agent Jim Stewart. We met during career day at the high school the year before last. I was just calling to see how things were going. Do you have any plans?"

"What...?"

"Listen," Stewart said, not giving Jeff time to respond, "let's not talk on the phone. Is there any chance we can meet, have a cup of coffee?"

"Sure. I guess so."

"Good. There's a little Cuban restaurant on Eighth Street called the Gire Sobre. You familiar with it?"

"No, not really."

"It's on the corner of Eighth and Northwest 22nd. Meet me there at 7:30 tomorrow morning and, Jeff, don't tell anyone about this meeting."

"But I just started a new job and...."

"Call and tell them you'll be late. I promise you, it will be worth your while. And remember, tell no one."

"Sure. I'll be there."

"Who was that?" Jeff's dad asked.

"Nobody. Just some guy about a job."

Jeff had no trouble finding the restaurant, and he got there a little early. When he walked in, he immediately recognized Jim Stewart. He was neatly dressed and clean-shaven, with salt and pepper hair. He was sitting at a table with a short, balding man smoking a cigar. The heavy smell of smoke from Cuban cigars was everywhere. They were speaking Spanish when Jeff approached the table. They stopped and looked up at Jeff. The bald man continued speaking in Spanish.

"He is big. Looks very strong. But he is just a kid."

"I am twenty," Jeff answered in Spanish. "I'll be twenty-one in January."

"So," the man said in perfect English as he put out his cigar, "the kid speaks Spanish."

"It's hard to live your whole life in Miami and not speak Spanish," Jeff replied.

If Jeff was scared, he didn't let it show at all. He was always like that, cocky.

"Sit down," Jim Stewart said, motioning to an open chair. "This is Raul."

"I am pleased to meet you," Raul said to Jeff with a handshake. He then turned back to Stewart and in Spanish, said, "What can the kid do other than speak Spanish?"

"Jeff here recently dropped out of an Ivy League school. Engineering? Right, Jeff?"

"I plan to go back to school," Jeff said.

"Well, that's a good thing. And I hope you do. But what are you going to do in the meantime?"

"I've got a job working as a plumber's helper."

"Making what? $4.50? Five bucks an hour?" Jim leaned in and looked in Jeff's eyes intently. "How would you like to make some real money and help your country at the same time?"

"What do you mean?"

"When we first met, I was recruiting prospective college students for the FBI—planting seeds in their heads early, so that if they were any good, we could get them when they left college.

"I also work for other branches of our government. Now, since you left college…."

"But I plan on finishing."

"But since you don't have a degree, I can't offer you work directly with our government. I hope you do return to college. But until you do, Raul here is what we call an operative. He doesn't really work for any office within the Justice Department, but he *does* work for all of them. He is the one who *might* be hiring you."

Jeff turned and looked at the short Latino man.

"How much do you bench press?" Raul asked.

"315."

"How fast are you?"

"I run the 40 in 4.7. Are you looking for a helper or a linebacker?"

"I know you are smart, kid," Raul said, "but you're young. A little bit in the strength department might make up for naiveté. Is that what position you play, linebacker?"

"In high school, I played all over the place. But in college, I was a linebacker."

"Can you catch?"

"No. I guess I should have said I played every position which did not require me touching the ball."

"I never could figure out American football. I love watching Larry Csonka run the ball, but everything else is a mystery to me. Okay, kid, I'll give you a try. Be here Friday morning at 7 A.M., and we'll start you."

"But I have to work Friday. I just started a new job."

"Kid," Raul said, leaning on his elbows and speaking softly. "I'll pay you $300 every time I use you. Go to work today and quit your job. Call in sick Friday. Do whatever it takes, but be here Friday."

With that, Raul got up and switched tables. Soon, a group of four men and two women joined him.

Raul was a native of Havana and the son of a wealthy club owner. In its heyday, Cuba was the vacation spot for the elite of the United States and several other countries and a hangout for mafia figures. Then, a young lawyer by the name of Fidel Castro sought to overthrow the regime of Ruben Fulgencio Batista. While Batista was a dictator, Raul's father, Juan José, heard rumblings of Castro's intentions, including a Marxist Communist regime and nationalization of most of Cuba's industry. Juan José sold his nightclub and took his young son and daughter to Miami.

The Hispanic community in Miami in the 1950s and 1960s was almost totally Cuban, usually well educated and mostly professionals who fled from the Castro regime. Raul grew up with a very mixed notion of which was his country. While he was at the University of Miami, he came to the conclusion that he was an American who was born in Cuba. His affiliation with Jim Stewart was, however, not a matter of patriotic pride. It was more like a job he stumbled into because of who his father was, combined with an opportunity to make some money. Because of Juan José's connection with the underworld from his nightclub days in Havana, the Bureau approached him about helping with a matter in Miami. Raul, by then a man in his own right, figured in the covert plan. The excitement and intrigue made Raul feel alive. He was hooked. He worked with Stewart, who was then a field agent, for a few years. Eventually, the drug cartels became a matter of their own. Raul struck out on his own as an operative and eventually developed his own cell. He now demanded great rewards, financially, and great respect for his effectiveness.

"Listen," Jim Stewart said softly, yet intently to Jeff. "I am going to tell you this only once, so I hope it sticks. Don't tell anybody about this. You may be out drinking one night, and you think this will get you laid, and you'll want to tell her something to impress her.

"First off, she ain't going to believe you. You may chase her away because she thinks you're a liar. Second, chances are, if a girl is talking to you, she has already decided whether or not she's having sex with you. If you do talk, this could bite you in the ass in a big way."

So, Jeff left the restaurant and he kept his mouth shut…until he learned about the Family Jewels thirty years later. He did, however, start his new job. Deep inside, Jeff just did not believe anything he had heard. When he showed up for the meeting on Friday, Raul did not have a job for him, so he went to work, quietly. He did not want Raul to know he took the plumbing job. They would meet again on Monday, and every Monday, Wednesday, and Friday, unless Raul said otherwise.

Chapter Five

It was later in the day after wolfing down a sandwich before Jennifer pulled the newspaper out of her lab coat pocket and began looking at it. She perused the stories on the front page, and then, she began looking at other headlines. She didn't see anything earth-shattering, so she stuck the paper back in her pocket and went back dictating her notes. Jeff called on her cell phone again.

"We need to talk," he said. "It's important."

"I looked at the paper," Jennifer protested, "I didn't see anything that would get you so upset."

"Look at the story on the front page on the bottom right about the Family Jewels."

"What the hell are the Family Jewels?" she asked as she pulled out the paper and began reading. "What does it have to do with you? I don't see why you would be so...."

"You won't know what it is. I have never told you about it." Jeff was very agitated, almost panic-stricken.

"Well, would you like to meet for dinner?"

"I don't want to talk about this in public," Jeff said.

"Okay, I've some steaks thawing in the refrigerator."

"Okay," Jeff said. "What time are you going to be home?"

"You know, I think I'm feeling a bit ill right now. Perhaps, I should go home now."

"Okay, I'll see you in a few minutes."

Jeff hung up the phone and started preparing to go home. Jennifer had to sit and think for a while. What could possibly have Jeff so upset?

Jeff had to tell her the whole story. There were parts he could not remember. There were things he did not want to remember. At first, she didn't believe him. When she decided he was telling the truth, she then thought it was kind of cool. Then, she wondered how Jeff could call himself a good Christian and do the things he had done. Eventually, she thought Jeff had been a thug, no better than the people from which he was supposedly protecting the country. Then, it hit her like a punch in the gut.

"How could we have been married for thirty years, and you never tell me?"

"I couldn't, baby," he began pleading. "At first, it was to protect you. I was told not to say anything. After a while, I was so ashamed. Then, I think I just blocked it from my mind, as if it never happened."

"You didn't trust me?"

"No, baby, I trusted you, but...." He could not think of a single legitimate reason why he did not tell her, except shame. Jeff could not deal with all the things he had done. It was easier to block them from his memory.

Jennifer was tall. When they married, she was often referred to as "statuesque." But being married to Jeff was no picnic. He had what she called a "dark side." Early in their life together, she would relieve the stress with pot or alcohol. She gave that up when she got pregnant but still had to deal with the stress. She turned to the one drug that was always available: food. She became a stress eater. After thirty years of marriage, Jennifer was still an attractive woman, but she always struggled with her weight. When the stress of Jeff's previous life had been repressed, other stressors appeared. It was a constant battle of diet, exercise, and then binge eating. At times, she thought about leaving Jeff. But, she realized she had an addiction that would stay with her, whether she was with Jeff or not.

"Why did you wait until now to tell me this?" Jennifer asked.

"I couldn't tell you before. And besides, I quit before we got married."

"So that's when we needed to start being honest? At the wedding?"

"Would you have loved me if you knew?"

"I don't know. I don't know if I know who you are now. I don't know if I can believe you. I just don't know."

Shortly after the wedding, Jeff promised himself to live as if none of his previous life existed. They left Miami to start a new life. Jennifer was a registered nurse, but without a bachelor's degree. They agreed to move near the University of Florida, near the opposite end of the state, and she would get her bachelor's degree, and they would start over. Both of their kids, Jeff Jr. and Rose, were born in Gainesville, and Jeff got a job with Plumbco working in the warehouse. Jeff's position with the company got better and better—the proverbial rags to riches boy. He was now a big boss.

The kids grew up, got married, and moved away, never knowing about their dad. In fact, Jeff thought no one knew or ever would know…until he learned about the Family Jewels.

"Tell me what's got you so upset about the article?"

Jennifer was like that: methodical, logical, and analytical.

"I am afraid that if my past comes out, my present will be ruined—at work, at church, in the neighborhood, everywhere." The thought of people knowing about the life Jeff once led terrified him.

"Tell me what you know about these 'Family Jewels.' Why would the *New York Times* want them?"

"I don't know. I have never heard of them before."

"Do you think you are mentioned in them? By name?"

"I don't know."

"You said you were pretty sure you worked mostly for the DEA (Drug Enforcement Administration). Did you do anything for the CIA?"

"I don't know." Jeff was almost pleading now. "Maybe."

"I thought you told me that nobody you worked with even knew your name. Were there any records kept of your assignments that you knew about?"

"I don't think so."

"Okay. So, we don't really have anything to worry about, right? Is there any chance that the *Times* won't get the documents?"

"I don't know. The article made it sound like a done deal. The CIA just needs to turn them over. I don't know about any time frame."

Jennifer ran her hand through her husband's hair and looked him in the eyes.

"Baby, we don't have anything to worry about right now. And chances are, we won't have anything to worry about when the information is released."

"What you're saying makes sense. I guess it just stirred up a lot of memories, memories I thought were gone. I couldn't face the people—at church, or at work."

"Honey," she said with a soothing tone, "you were one of the good guys. You don't have anything to be ashamed of."

Jeff looked at her. There was a hint of a tear in his eye.

"There were no good guys."

Chapter Six

Jeff had been going to "meetings" for about two weeks before he got his first assignment. Since he was working in new construction, he would go from the meeting to the job site and be only a few minutes late. No one ever noticed. Nobody ever said anything. On the day he received his first assignment, he called in sick to the plumbing company.

There was a particularly bloodthirsty drug gang operating out of Colombia that had set up shop in Miami. The Median Cartel was extremely violent when it came to competitors, mostly Cubans. What made things worse was their disregard for innocent bystanders. The thug in charge of the Miami operation was twenty-four-year-old Colombian named Carlos Sanchez, known as the Crow. Supposedly, the head of the cartel back in Colombia knew how vicious and careless Sanchez could be, and that was why he was in Miami.

The body of a young black prostitute had been found in a posh hotel in Miami Beach, and the company left it to Raul to pin

her murder on Sanchez. She had been tortured and strangled—
that would certainly sound like the Crow.

"Listen, we know the Crow probably didn't do this," Raul
told the men gathered at the table, "but there's a whole lot of
other stuff we know Carlos did do. Police don't know about this
hooker yet. We've got until this afternoon to get the evidence and
place it at the scene.

"Kid, do you own a suit?"

"I can get one, quick," Jeff responded.

"Okay, go get a haircut, too. If you clean up a little bit, you'd
look like a cop.

"Bernie," he said to an overweight Latin man with a crew cut,
"wear that plaid jacket and that ugly ass tie I always kid you
about. Both of you guys, leave your .45s at home. I'll have a
couple of .38 specials. Meet me at the Causeway at 1 P.M."

Raul had given Jeff a Smith & Wesson .45 automatic. He
pointed out that at the time (the 1970s) police were still carrying
revolvers, which only had six shots before they needed to be re-
loaded. Most of the Fed's and all Raul's people carried .45s with
a twenty-shot clip.

Raul then turned to Jeff. "This will be easy, kid. Just pick up
things without the Crow seeing you that we can plant for evidence. It's gotta be things he'd take with him to see a hooker, and
it's gotta have his fingerprints on it."

Raul turned to Bernie. "This will be the first time out for the
kid. Don't sweat it too much, but keep an eye on him. You keep
the Crow busy while the kid is pocketing stuff."

When Jeff showed up at the Causeway, Raul and Bernie were
waiting with what looked like an unmarked police car. Bernie was

going to begin questioning the Crow as if the girl's body had already been discovered, and he was a suspect. While the questioning was going on, all Jeff had to do was pocket two or three things that might have the Crow's fingerprints without putting his own prints on the "evidence."

When Jeff and Bernie arrived, Carlos came out and met them. He was wearing a pair of dark-colored, pleated pants, an unbuttoned dress shirt with a "wife beater" underneath, and a pair of platform shoes. He had a five o'clock shadow, and it wasn't quite noon.

"What the hell do you guys want?"

"I'm Detective Sgt. Mack James, and this is…."

"I can see you're freaking cops. I ain't blind. What do you want?"

"Mr. Sanchez, have you ever seen this woman?" Bernie handed the Crow a photo of the dead hooker.

"She ain't my type."

"Well, we have reason to believe you have been with her recently."

Carlos motioned them over to a table and chairs on the front porch. They weren't surprised not to be invited in, but Jeff knew he could pick up better stuff inside the house. Carlos lit a cigar and laid the lighter on the table. Bernie moved around to Carlos's right and, when the Crow followed him with his head, Jeff picked up the lighter in a tissue and placed it in his coat pocket.

Another man approached the table. He was big and had huge, muscular arms and a flabby gut that jiggled as he walked. Jeff thought he must have been put together from spare parts, Frankenstein's Monster.

"Everything okay, Boss?" the creep asked in Spanish.

Bernie responded in Spanish, "We're just talking to Mr. Sanchez," as he flashed the new man a badge.

"I think we're done talking," Carlos said as he put his cigar out in the ashtray.

Bernie stepped in front of the drug lord and said, "Where were you from 10 P.M. last night until 10 A.M. this morning?"

Carlos's hired man stepped into the fray, and Jeff took the opportunity to pick up the cigar in another tissue and stick it in his other pocket. He then joined in the shoving match.

"I'm not saying a fucking thing without my attorney."

"Let's head to the house," Jeff said. Then, looking at Bernie, he added, "I think Mr. Sanchez has given us all we need."

Bernie and Jeff rushed back to meet with Raul, and Raul got the evidence to the room before allowing a hotel maid to find the body. The frame-up began.

"What do we expect to gain from this?" Jeff asked the two men.

"We don't ask those questions," Bernie said. "We just carry out the plan. Stay focused on the plan, and you'll be okay. Just do your job."

"Bernie's right," Raul said. "We don't ask questions, but I'll tell you…this time.

"If we can make it look like the Crow committed this murder, then at best, he'll be convicted and sent away. At worst, he'll be deported. If we raise enough of a storm, the cartel may summon him back to Colombia. In any case, we get one mean, violent son of a bitch off the streets and out of our hair."

"How about the hooker—her real killer?"

"We know who that is," Raul said. It was obvious the conversation was over.

Chapter Seven

Jeff woke up, sweating. It was 2:30 A.M. He did not know what woke him—a dream or a noise—but he was wide awake. A thousand things were running through his head.

What was in the Family Jewels?

Who compiled them?

What if Fr. Bob and the people at church found out?

What if the people at work or his customers found out? Would they fire him?

After lying in bed for an hour, awake and restless, Jeff got up and searched through his wife's drugs. He knew she had plenty of alprazolam, a sedative prescribed for her anxiety. He took one and had a glass of wine, just to ensure sleep. He was out in twenty minutes. However, when the alarm went off at 6 A.M., Jeff had a hard time getting out of bed. He got Jennifer her coffee, eventually, but he wasn't early for work that day, and his attitude was noticeably different. His coworkers thought there might be a problem at home. Maybe, since Jeff left early the previous day, he was coming down with something. Jeff knew it was the drugs.

At least, he was pretty sure it was the drugs. He trudged through the day. The odd thing was that Jeff loved his job, but he just did not want to be there that day. He didn't want to call on customers or deal with other people's problems. He took sales orders and wrote invoices, but even those tasks seemed to be almost overwhelming.

And he felt like Roger was watching him, evaluating his performance. What was Roger thinking?

Chapter Eight

The plan was working. Carlos Sanchez was a suspect in the murder of Tamika Marx. There was evidence that placed him at the scene of the crime, and he had no solid alibi for that evening. He had a high-powered attorney, but Raul's people bugged his office. Things looked good for the good guys. It was time to leave that pot to stew for a while and move on to something else.

But Jeff also got some grief from his other job, and from home.

"Why didn't you go to work yesterday?" his dad asked. "Where were you all day?"

"What do you mean?" Obviously, someone told his father something.

"They called here, said you called in sick. They said you called after everyone had already left for the job site. What did you do all day?"

For his part in the Crow operation, Jeff received $600, a lot of money for a twenty-year-old male in 1977. With the $600 he received for his first job, Jeff planned to move out of his parents' house and get a place of his own. His parents were only slightly concerned on those nights Jeff didn't come home, but it was time to be on his own. The only problem was that Jeff was twenty years old. Of the first $600 Jeff earned, he spent $100 on a gram of cocaine, another $50 on a bag of pot, and countless drinks for one pretty young woman who fell for Jeff's looks and whose name he completely forgot. By the end of the evening, Jeff bought another gram of cocaine, a bottle of champagne for the beautiful girl, which she threw up before Jeff was done with her, and a lot of booze for himself. Jeff was broke. He would be more careful with his second payment. He would go directly to his new landlord and pay the first month's rent and security deposit on a one-bedroom apartment. He would be happy then.

"I, I just didn't feel like working," Jeff finally stammered to his father.

"Listen, son, as long as you're living in this house...."

"Oh, bullshit, Dad," Jeff said as he stood up, his fists clenched in rage. He was not intending to use them, but his father leapt to his feet, and the two men stood, face to face, sizing up each other. Bill and Jeff Murdock were the same height. Bill was decidedly bigger than his son, but Jeff was all muscle.

It could be said that if you look up "dysfunctional family" in the dictionary, you will find a picture of the Murdock family. Bill Murdock's father, Gus, died when Bill was eleven. The older Murdock worked in a lumber mill in South Carolina near the end of the Great Depression. One chilly morning, he put on a flannel shirt over his work shirt while he and another man were loading wood into a planer. Gus was not the neatest man, and he was often accused of being careless. That morning, he did not button the sleeves of the flannel shirt. The planer grabbed the flapping material and pulled Gus into the grinding, cutting teeth. The machine ground to a halt, but it had to be shut down and dismantled in order to get Gus out. By the time his body was free, life had long since left it.

In the early 1930s, there was no Social Security, no death benefits, and no widow's pension. The owner of the mill gave Gus's widow—Bill's mother—$100. That was a lot of money for 1934, but it was not enough to care for her, Bill, his sister, and his two brothers. One of the boys was less than a year old.

They were always a handful, and it was difficult for the young mother to find work with so many kids to care for. Bill and his older brother, Gus Junior, were always getting into fights, with each other or with other teenagers. When Bill reached the ripe old age of seventeen, his mother went with him to sign the necessary papers for Bill to enter the Navy in January of 1942. Gus Junior joined, also, but he did not need his mother's signature. Bill often wondered in those early years if his mother was sending him off to war because she did not have a babysitter. The only man Bill had as a father figure was an ill-tempered chief petty officer who did not hesitate to use physical force to ensure the sailors under him carried out orders. This was the model of discipline Bill took into fatherhood.

Jo, Bill's wife and Jeff's mother, was the most neurotic woman Jeff had ever encountered. One of three sisters, she came from an alcoholic father and a mother who took out the pent-up rage she felt for her husband on her three daughters. Despite the fact he could not go one day without drinking, Jo Murdock's father was a taxi driver. He had at least two one-car accidents in which he was drinking, but it was a small town and a time when police and the public would turn their heads. Still, it was not driving and drinking that killed Jo's dad. Instead, he parked his cab in front of the house one night and never came in. The next morning, Jo's mother found him slumped over, dead. He apparently died of a combination of alcohol poisoning and liver failure.

After her father's death, her mother became noticeably easier to live with. This sent a very confusing message to Jo. She was already seventeen years old, so Jo was already formed into an abusive mother, but her understanding of marital relations, imperfect from the years of witnessing her parents fight it out, was now even more distorted into believing outliving a bad husband was the key to happiness.

Bill and Jo Murdock's oldest son, Will or "Junior" as they called him, bore the brunt of his violent parents. Once caught smoking, they made Junior eat an entire pack of cigarettes. Each time he was overheard using what they considered foul language, they made him bite in half a new bar of soap. That's not to say he would escape a beating for those crimes. The creative lesson learning was in addition to "good old-fashioned disciple." To escape the abuse, Junior married a girl he barely knew within weeks after his graduation. His plan was to get enough cash in wedding gifts to setup a new apartment, and it worked. The only problem was that within a month after the wedding, Junior's new wife realized she had made a mistake. Within three months, she filed for divorce. But Junior kept the apartment. He lived his life after that drinking, smoking pot, experimenting with various drugs, and going from one meaningless relationship to another. He was, by this time, on the payroll at his father's plumbing company, and Bill kept him on, though Junior did not always get a full week of work.

The next son, Buster, was about a year older than Jeff. Buster was intelligent, but not really book smart. He had a lot of common sense, but did not do well in school or with tests. Buster's escape was simple: when he turned eighteen, he moved out. He had his own car, which he paid for working part-time in the lounge at a country club. He moved in with Junior and worked as many hours at the country club as he could while working on graduating high school six months later. He lived with Junior for a couple of years until Junior allowed a runaway girl younger than Buster to move in with them. Buster knew the girl was cute, but also thought she was crazy. He got another roommate.

Jeff recalled the first time, the only time he ever hit his father. He was fifteen or sixteen years old at the time. One afternoon, Jeff's mother got extremely angry with him, as she often did, and began slapping him with both hands, as she often did. At first, Jeff simply blocked her attempts. Finally, he grabbed her wrists and yelled, "Will you please stop!"

"You just wait 'til I tell your father," she said as she left the room, sobbing.

When Bill Murdock arrived home that night, his wife told him that Jeff had hit her. He was furious. Jeff was in the kitchen when Bill came up behind him. Bill began punching and kicking Jeff in an uncontrolled rage.

"Hit me!" he kept screaming. "You think you can hit your mother, come on and hit me!"

Jeff was in a defensive position and was forced back into a corner. As Jeff replayed this scene in his head, he wasn't sure if it was the beating or the berating, but Jeff, squatting in the corner, finally had enough. At sixteen, he was much smaller than his father. He knew he would only get this chance once. Jeff planted his foot in the corner, where the counter, the wall, and the floor met, and he launched himself, just like he was doing squats in the weight room, and exploded out of the corner, landing a punch somewhere on Bill Murdock's face that sent him stumbling backwards until he fell on the opposite side of the kitchen, diagonally from Jeff.

Jeff recalled how Bill slowly stood up, rubbing his face and looking at Jeff.

Jeff stood there, sixteen years old and all of 190 pounds, with a clenched fist, just like today. He was not going to cower in the corner anymore.

On the positive side, all of the extremely violent beatings stopped that day. But a negative effect that Jeff would not figure out until years later was the guilt he carried from then on. Jeff's two older brothers moved out as soon as they could to escape their father's brand of discipline. They both were scarred for life. Jeff's younger brothers and his younger sister would not have to endure the number of years of slapping, kicking, and punching that the older three had. Jeff began to believe, deep in his heart, that if he would have only hit his father sooner, it would have saved everyone a lot of suffering.

Jeff reached back and grabbed the doorknob without taking his eyes off of his father. When the door was open, Jeff quickly backed out. While he was bigger and stronger now than he was at sixteen, Jeff had always known that it was the surprise in his punch that caught his father, not the power. As he walked away from the house, Jeff began to ponder if he should quit the plumbing job.

Raul trusted Jeff now. Jeff didn't talk much, quit asking questions, and implemented some creative thinking when needed to get a job done. Raul now understood what Jim Stewart saw in Jeff. He was an asset. The good thing was that Jeff could think. Raul also knew that smart people could be a problem, too. Sometimes it is better not to ask questions and just follow the plan.

Chapter Nine

When Jeff went into Jerry's Plumbing the next day, his plan was to quit.

"Hey, we missed you the other day," the young woman said as Jeff walked into the shop. "You all better?"

"Hey, Peg. Yeah, I'm fine." Peg, or Margaret, as her father called her, seemed genuinely interested. She graduated from the same Catholic high school as Jeff. When she, the daughter of the wealthy plumbing contractor, was in school, she had little to do with the son of a service plumber who struggled to make ends meet. Jeff wasn't sure if the concern indicated she cared, or if she was playing the role of employer. "Is your father here?"

"No, he and mom are out of town for a few days. Gone to a convention of some sort."

"Oh," Jeff was unsure of what to do next.

"Is there something I can help you with?" Peg's light-blue eyes twinkled, her creamy colored face framed by her black hair, cut a little longer than a pageboy.

"Well," Jeff said, "I am just wondering if this job is for me...."

"Oh, Jeff," Peg said, "you're not thinking about quitting, are you?"

She stepped forward and put her hand on Jeff's muscular chest. He didn't know if she could feel his heart beating, but he could. She was petite, maybe five foot two. As she stared up into Jeff's eyes from a foot shorter, Jeff noticed how perfect her breasts were, how clear and soft her skin was, and how beautiful she was. Jeff had admired her from afar in high school, but knew she was out of his league.

"Dad says you're one of the hardest workers we've ever had. I know it would hurt him if you quit, and it would crush me."

"Well, it's just that…."

"I'll tell you what. Mom and dad are out of town tonight, and I'm all by myself. Why don't you come over and have supper with me, and maybe I can…persuade you to stay."

"Well, okay," Jeff said.

Peg slid her hand up Jeff's chest and wrapped it around the back of his neck and stroked his hair.

"You know where the house is?"

"Sure."

"Great. I'll see you at about seven." She gave Jeff a quick peck on the cheek and headed up the stairs to the office. Jeff couldn't help but watch her cute butt cheeks bounce along behind her.

"You want a camera?" a coworker asked as the crews started walking to the trucks. "Let's go."

When Jeff arrived at the house, Peg was scurrying about the kitchen. To Jeff's surprise, she was wearing a bikini.

"Come on in," she said. "Dinner is ready."

The table was set, and the food was ready to be served.

"What's with the bathing suit?" Jeff asked with a grin, "I mean, not that I mind or anything. You look great!"

"Thank you," Peg smiled. "I just thought maybe we'd go swimming after we eat."

"Oh," Jeff said as he assumed the seat at the head of the table. He didn't think about his boss having a swimming pool. He did not bring a bathing suit, but he just let that go for now.

As they ate and drank wine, the two young people talked about everything and anything, except why Jeff was there. The possibility of him leaving Jerry's Plumbing never came up.

After dinner, Peg rose said, "I'll go get us some more wine, and I'll meet you out by the pool."

Jeff walked out to the pool and stood there, awkwardly waiting.

Peg walked out and handed him his glass of wine.

"Afraid of the water?" she asked.

"No," Jeff said. "It's just that I did not bring a suit or shorts or anything."

Peg glided over and turned off the light. She returned in the same fluid motion to stand in front of Jeff. He could see her clearly in the fading Florida light as she reached behind her neck with her right hand and behind her back with her left hand and untied her bikini top. She held it up in her right hand, her firm breasts displayed in all their beauty.

"If you don't wear one, I won't wear one."

Jeff was so anxious and reckless removing his clothes. He could have fallen and spilt his head on the concrete.

"Calm down, Big Boy," Peg said as she took Jeff over to the steps of the pool and had him sit on the top step. His ass was in the water. Peg was able to take him in her mouth and still be above the water so that she could breathe. Jeff was feeling the urge to cum, but at the same time unable due to the coolness of the water. After several minutes, they changed positions. Jeff had to work a little harder to get air, but the cool water did not prevent Peg from reaching a screaming climax, which Jeff feared might draw the attention of neighbors. To Jeff's surprise, she came a second time. This time, Peg bit her lip and stifled her screams of passion.

They made love in the pool, and Jeff rethought the need to quit Jerry's Plumbing.

Chapter Ten

Jeff walked into the restaurant where he was to meet Jack Butler, a longtime plumber in Gainesville. Butler had a couple of big jobs coming up: a hospital and two housing developments where his company was doing all the plumbing in all the houses. Jeff was surprised to see his coworker, Terry, sitting at the table with Butler.

"What's this?" Jeff asked.

"Oh, Terry and I were just talking over some old times," Butler said.

"You aren't trying to take over one of my customers, are you?"

The look on Jeff's face was hard to read. Was he joking, or did he really think Terry was trying to take away a big account.

"Oh, come on," Terry said smiling, "Jack and I go way back. We went to high school together. You don't really think I'd be...."

"Of course, he doesn't," Jack Butler said. "He's just pulling your leg."

Jeff began to wonder if Butler was in on the conspiracy. He sat down uneasily. For a short while, Jeff did all he could to make

Terry feel unwelcomed without being too conspicuous. At least, Jeff thought he was not conspicuous. When Terry's customer walked in, he got up and sat with them.

"Well, that was a bit uncomfortable," Butler said.

"Yeah. The nerve of that guy."

"I'm not talking about Terry," Butler said. "I'm talking about you. I'm your customer because Roger tells me you're the best. But I have known Terry for a hell of a long time. This is not a case of you versus him. You've got enough competition outside your company without worrying about Terry. You just focus on getting me the best deals for my supplies."

That was it. Jeff knew. Terry had been talking to Jack and Roger about making Butler one of Terry's accounts.

As time went on, Jeff was sleeping less and less. He was drinking more and dipping into his wife's alprazolam two or three times a week. His behavior was becoming erratic. Mary, in the office, used to flirt openly with Jeff. Now, she avoided him.

Jeff was also becoming less effective. His sales were slipping. He did not come in as early as he once did, but he still read the paper every morning. He would occasionally stay late, but it was only to complete things he should have completed during the day. He no longer enjoyed his job as he once did, but he could not figure out why everyone and everything around him was changing.

Chapter Eleven

"We have to empty this building," Raul told the crew he had assembled. Jeff's hair has started to grow long again, but Raul said it didn't matter. He was dressed in a postal delivery uniform. "Kid, you go in and deliver this package. It's a bomb."

Everyone at the table recoiled a bit.

"Don't worry. It's a real bomb, C-4 explosives and all. But the alarm clock is not set. The connection to the battery will never be complete. After the kid has been out of the building for twenty-five minutes, if they have not called the police, I'll call in a bomb to the cops. Once they empty the building, company people will come in and do what they have to do."

"What's that?" Jeff asked.

"You were getting so good at not asking questions," Raul said. "Just keep moving. Go around the corner, and I'll be waiting there for you. Just remember, we have to get there before the real mail carrier."

The previous day, a couple of Raul's people had gotten their hands on about half the mail destined for the Dade Credit Union

Building. The building housed offices for attorneys, financial planners, accountants, and a multitude of other professionals. The mail was delivered to a central location—a mail room—and then sorted for each tenant. Jeff delivered the mail, including a parcel addressed to a law firm in the building. He walked out onto the street and passed the building next door. Around the corner sat a white mail truck with Raul behind the wheel on the right-hand side. Jeff rolled up the back door, laid down his shoulder bag full of fake mail, and climbed in. He closed the door behind him.

"Let's don't wait here," Raul said. "Larry's across the street. If they don't find it in twenty minutes, he'll call and tell them it's there."

In the bank building, the mailroom people did not recognize the name on the box and just set it aside. A supervisor walked in and asked, "What's this?"

"Wrong address," a skinny little man said.

The beefy supervisor picked up the box, shook it, and listened.

"I don't like this," he said. "Better open it up."

The scrawny man took a box cutter and opened the package. Inside were a battery, an alarm clock, and some wires going into a big wad of plastic explosives.

"Oh, shit," both men said simultaneously.

The building was empty in less than fifteen minutes. The Bomb Squad and Fire Department were there in a flash, along with the company men waiting at the corner. During the confusion, they went in and did whatever it was they were going to do. Jeff never learned what that was, but it was the easiest $400 he had ever made.

Chapter Twelve

In early June, the Federal Government turned the Family Jewels over to the *New York Times*. It was 700 pages of documents, narratives, invoices, and a compilation of data that would take months to sort.

Jeff remembered the only person other than Jennifer with whom he had discussed his past: Fr. John. Jeff's life had changed, slowly but completely. Jeff always thought of himself as a good Catholic boy. It never occurred to him that in his younger days, he drank, smoked pot, occasionally snorted cocaine, and had sex rather indiscriminately, and those are contrary to the teachings of the Church. He just knew that he had always believed in God. He would reason, "Isn't that good enough?" He could rationalize anything and justify everything. In his mind, his behavior was acceptable. He blamed it on the physical abuse he endured in the name of discipline, on having to share everything with his four brothers and one sister, on anything he could think of short of accepting the blame. Then, he began to look at his life, especially when he and his young bride moved to Gainesville. They agreed it would be a better place and a better way to raise their children. Still, Jeff's conversion was an evolution, not a revolution.

"Bless me, Father, for I have sinned. It has only been a few weeks since my last confession, but I have something I want to…I need to get off my chest."

"What is it, Jeff?" Fr. John asked.

Jeff had lived in Gainesville for about six years at the time, and he had been attending St. Martin's from the start. At first, he and Jennifer and the kids went only occasionally, but it grew into a weekly family thing. Jeff was now a reader, and Jennifer taught Sunday school.

"The thing is, Father, the sins I want to talk about are ten years old. I have been to confession several times since then, and every time I had the intention of talking about them…," Jeff looked down and rubbed his hands together, "…every time, though, I chickened out. I just couldn't bring myself to talk about them."

"They must be pretty bad."

"The thing is, I always thought I was doing the right thing. I always thought I was a good guy."

"Okay," Fr. John said. "Start from the beginning. Chances are, you are not going to tell me anything I haven't heard before."

The litany started. Jeff told him everything. He cried. He sobbed. Some of it Jeff could barely say. But he told him everything.

"Well," Fr. John said, "I guess now I've heard just about everything.

"But let me ask you, why didn't you bring this to the confessional before? I mean, it's obvious to me that you regret them. You seem truly contrite. Why did you wait?"

"I don't know. The longer I waited, the harder it got to say anything."

"My guess is that God forgave you a long time ago for any wrong you did. The real sin, the real problem, is that you have waited so long to deal with this. I don't know if keeping these emotions bottled up inside of you is a good thing. You need to deal with it."

"I guess that's true," Jeff said.

"Would you like to make an appointment to talk with me about this, or would you rather go to a mental health professional?"

Jeff made an appointment with Fr. John.

When he left the church that night, Jeff felt better, much better. He now realized he was forgiven, that he had been forgiven. For those ten years before his confession, he had not forgiven himself. He now had a spring in his step, and he smiled.

He cancelled the appointment with Fr. John the day before they were to meet. Fr. John was reassigned six months later, and he took Jeff's secret with him.

Jeff never again spoke of his past, and he resealed the bottle.

Chapter Thirteen

After about three months with Raul's cell, Jeff was carrying more weaponry. He always had his .45 tucked in the back of his pants or in the big pocket inside his jean jacket. He went so far as to cut the sleeves off so he could wear the denim vest even when it was hot. Jeff also carried a switchblade in his back pocket next to his wallet and carried a MAC-10 for the really dangerous jobs. A MAC-10 is an automatic weapon, about fifteen inches long, and the clip is the handle, so the gun can be made very compact and easy to conceal. The clip holds about thirty rounds, and the MAC-10 fires fifteen rounds per second. If you hold the trigger for two seconds, you empty the clip. He picked up the MAC-10 off the body of a cocaine cowboy killed in a shootout. Jeff had never fired a gun at any human, and he had never been shot at. The weapons made him feel safer, but he wasn't sure he'd be able to shoot another person.

Until he had to.

Oddly enough, Jeff's first exchange of gunfire had nothing to do with company work, other than where he was. Raul wanted to talk with a few of his guys one evening at the Gire Sobre, and it was late when Jeff was leaving.

"Give me your wallet, now!" the young voice screamed at Jeff from behind. He heard the hammer pulled back and locked. Jeff's instincts took over. He dropped to the ground and spun to his right, pulling out his .45 as he went down.

The young, would-be robber fired his gun. With Jeff now facing his assailant, the shot went to his right. Jeff shot back and hit the boy—a black kid not more than sixteen—right in the gut.

Raul and Larry came running.

"What the hell's going on?" Larry yelled. Raul was calm.

"I'm okay," Jeff said. "This kid took a shot at me. He was trying to rob me."

Now, Jeff's heart was racing. Larry started to tend to the robber as he lay on the ground.

"Leave him," Raul said. "Medics will be here soon. We've got to get out of here."

Jeff got out of his crouched position.

"You're bleeding," Larry said.

"Looks like his shot ricocheted off that car," Raul observed, "and hit you in the ass. Get in my car."

The three men left the scene before the Miami Police arrived. The feds had a medical crew that took care of company men in this situation. The patients were often agents, but always discreet. Raul made a call, and some people met them at Dade Medical Plaza near the Federal Building. In just a few minutes, Jeff was laying on his stomach on a gurney in the emergency room. His pants and boxers were around his knees.

"Nice ass," the woman assisting the doctor laughed, "but it's got a hole in it."

Despite the pain and humiliation, Jeff was flattered.

"Actually, it has two," the doctor smirked. "It's supposed to have one.

"You know, if any other operative had called me, I'd tell them to go to hell. You're lucky you were with Raul," he added. "How'd you say you got this?"

"Ricochet," Jeff started.

"We were working on the Carlos Sanchez thing," Raul leapt in. "Had a small exchange of gunfire. No one else got hit."

"You're lucky it was a ricochet," the doctor said. "The slug kind of flattened out, which made the wound bigger, but it's not deep. The loss of velocity and wider area worked in your favor."

He plunked the slug into a metal bedpan.

"Three, oh," he said to the woman, indicating the thread size for sutures.

"Sure thing, Doc," she said. "Try and leave a little bit of a scar. Chicks dig scars."

She moved around where she could make eye contact with Jeff. She winked one of her blue eyes at Jeff as she tucked some blonde hair behind an ear. Despite her fair features, she was obviously Latina. She smiled, and Jeff smiled back.

"Easy now, kid," the doctor said. "Let me sew this thing up before you get those hormones flowing or they'll spill out all over the floor."

Jeff didn't get to know the girl any better, but he would see her from time to time in or near the Federal Building. But he would never forget that face.

Chapter Fourteen

When Jeff arrived at Plumbco that morning, Mary was waiting in his office.

"Mr. Murdock, we need to talk."

"Mary," he said, "what's with this Mr. Murdock crap?" He was puzzled. "What happened to Jeff?"

"That's what I'd like to know."

"Huh?"

"Jeff, you're just not the same person I used to work for. Something has happened these past few months. You have changed."

"What do you mean? How?"

"I don't know, or I just don't want to talk about it. I just think it's time for a change."

"What do you mean?"

"I've taken a job in a law office. I'm giving my two week's notice."

"What?" Jeff felt a mixture of emotions: sadness, anger, hurt, but mostly, he was perplexed. "Did Roger do something? Is he chasing you away?"

"You see! That's what I mean!" she said at the verge of tears. "You always blame someone else. You never see how insane you are acting. You don't act like the Jeff who hired me."

"Mary, please don't go. I'll work on getting the old Jeff back. I promise."

By now, Mary was at full sob. She looked at Jeff with red eyes, tears streaming down her face. Jeff was gaunt, his hair uncombed, and he shaved only sporadically. "It's too late," she said, and she darted out of the office and into the ladies room. When she finally came out of the restroom, she went straight to her car and left. She called the receptionist on her cell phone and told her she was going home, sick.

Jeff didn't feel too well, either.

When he arrived home, Jennifer and the two kids were waiting for him in the living room.

"Jeff, Rose, what are you guys doing here?" he asked.

"Dad," Jeff Jr. started, "Mom's worried about you. We're all worried about you."

"What? Why?"

"Dear," Jennifer said, putting her hand on Jeff's arm, "Sit down. I think it's about time we tell the kids."

"Told them what?"

"Dear, you have not been yourself since that story came out in the paper...."

"Oh, no, we are not talking about that!"

"Talking about what?" Rose asked. "What story?"

"Dad, you have been really weird lately," Jeff Jr. said.

"I will not. I cannot talk about this," Jeff insisted.

"Jeff, honey, please listen," Jennifer started, "you need to talk to somebody. I want to make an appointment for you with Len."

Len Stockholm was a psychologist and counselor who had worked with Jeff and Jennifer about marriage issues in the past and with Jennifer on her stress issues.

"No, dear. I don't need to see him."

"Dad," Jeff Jr. said, "you need to do something. You should see yourself right now."

Jeff had literally backed into a corner of the room and was assuming a defensive position, as if he was going to fight his way out. For a second, for a brief instant, he realized the absurdity of his position. He stood up straight, dropped his hands, and relaxed a little bit.

"Okay," he said. "I'll go see Len." That night, Jeff had a dream. He was sitting in Len's office, talking. He made a comment to Len about a fight he was in one night in Miami Beach—truly an ass kicking. He told Len of how he had been beaten by six or seven guys. Jeff had been hit in the face a couple of times with brass knuckles and over the back with a folding metal chair. He told Len what he remembered most was the profuse amount of blood puddled around him and having the knowledge that it was all his. Then, in a perplexing twist to the dream, he was no longer in Len's office, but in the fight. Blood covered his feet and the ground around him, and he refused to be knocked down.

When Jeff awoke, he tried to interpret the dream. He believed it had something to do with going to Len's office. He decided therapy was a bad idea. He went to his first appointment with

Len, but did not share with him the details that concerned his wife, his kids, and his former secretary. They were all imagining things.

Chapter Fifteen

"I don't really know what to expect in there tonight," Raul said to Jeff as he drove him down Seventh Avenue. "There is no legal connection between the bar 'El Cuervo' and Carlos Sanchez, but there is no doubt he does business from there."

Jeff could not help but wonder if the bar was named after Carlos, the Crow, or if Carlos was named after the bar.

"You don't think he'll recognize me? From the cop scam?" Jeff asked.

"Your hair has already grown back almost to your shoulders, and the facial hair makes you look totally different. Wear the baseball cap, and I'll guarantee he won't recognize you. Besides, I doubt he'll be there tonight. We just want a layout of the place."

"I can't believe you've known about this joint all along, and you haven't gone inside."

"It's just not a wise thing for me to do. Here. I'll drop you off here, and walk the rest of the way. Look around. Don't stay more than a half an hour. I'll pick you up here when you're done."

Jeff didn't like the idea of walking a block on this street alone in Miami, especially since the incident at the Gire Sobre. He had his .45 and his switchblade. He would be okay.

He walked into El Cuervo and sat at the bar. He could only hear Spanish being spoken, and the place grew noticeably quieter when he walked in. The Colombian bartender walked up to him.

"What do you want?" he asked in English with bit of a sneer on his face.

"Cerveza," Jeff said. When he worked at it, his accent was very Cuban.

The conversation resumed. Jeff got his beer and took a sip as he threw three one-dollar bills on the counter for his $2 beer. He looked around and made a few more mental notes. The building was a big rectangle, made of concrete block which was not stuccoed, but was painted. There was a paneled dividing wall more than three-quarters of the way back with a large opening in it. The restrooms were back there. When he finished the beer, Jeff sought out the restroom, pretending to be looking for it as he was taking in more of El Cuervo. There were two offices in the back. That's more than a small joint like this would need. Jeff saw a storage room with a steel door and padlock that would be acceptable as a bank vault in some South American towns. The wall to the storage room was concrete block, but not painted. That meant it had been put in later. Someone came out of the men's room, and Jeff stepped in to avoid suspicion. He returned to find his seat at the bar was still available.

A Colombian man, much smaller than Jeff, came and sat down next to him and peered at him.

"This guy is a pig!" the Colombian yelled.

The bar fell quiet.

"What the fuck are you talking about?" Jeff asked in Spanish. He began to think. *Was he at the Crow's house that day? Who is this?*

"I saw you with Raul Gutierez!"

"Who?"

"The DEA man, you pig! I saw you with him!"

"I don't know what you're talking about."

"I saw you with him earlier tonight in a car."

Jeff thought quickly.

"I don't know any Raul. Some guy gave me a ride, and when I wouldn't have sex with him, he made me get out of the car."

The bartender snickered.

The smaller Colombian was pointing his finger in Jeff's face. Jeff reached over and grabbed him by the shirt collar. He soon wished he had not.

The little man brought both hands up and knocked Jeff's hands away. He then hit Jeff with his left hand twice, quick as lightning, and then with his right. It felt like Jeff had been smashed in the face by a hammer, and he staggered back a step or two, his nose bleeding and a cut above his left eye.

Jeff knew two things: 1) This little guy is a boxer, and 2) Jeff could not let him land another punch.

Too late. Another right and blood was now streaming from Jeff right eyebrow and dripping from his nose. He had to think quick.

Jeff let his football instincts take over. He rushed to the little man, running hard and low. When he made contact, he continued running until he smacked into the concrete block wall. The Colombian softened Jeff's impact.

Jeff then rolled to the little man's left as he grabbed his shirt again and, with all of his might, swung the little man from his left to his right until he made contact with the wall, shoulder first, but his head slapped into the block. Jeff then swung him back to where he started. This time, contact was head first, and the blood splattered, getting some on Jeff. Better make sure. Jeff swung him back the other way again; this time like a sack of potatoes. His feet swung limply out in the air as he once again slapped into the wall and blood splattered everywhere. Jeff dropped him there. When he looked out into the bar, the whole crowd was staring at him.

"Holy shit," one man said, "he beat the shit out of Javier."

Jeff bent over and picked up his cap. At first, he thought the whole bar was going to jump on him. He had his hand ready to pull out his .45, but he realized nobody was moving. He staggered toward the door and headed to his rendezvous point.

"What the hell happened to you?" Raul asked.

"I got made. It's okay, though. I talked my way out of it."

Blood was dripping from Jeff's face, and his shirt and denim jacket were covered in blood, a mixture of Jeff's and Javier's.

"You think so, huh?" Raul said, handing him a tissue. The whole sequence seemed so ridiculous. They both laughed.

"Okay, I guess it's time to go see the Doc again," Raul suggested.

Jeff began dabbing at the cut above his eye uselessly with the tissue. He finally decided to just apply pressure. He began to wonder, what made him keep fighting? He was getting his ass whooped. Nobody would blame him if he ran. He thought, chances are nobody would have let me out the door. Jeff knew he was a little meaner than the average guy. Some might even call him "bloodthirsty."

He remembered a time when he was younger.

Jeff and his older brother fought a lot, even for siblings. Their father, being a harsh disciplinarian, created his own way of curbing their fighting. He would take the two into the backyard and make them fight. If one quit fighting, Bill Murdock would come and hit them with a belt until they started fighting again. This punishment worked to keep the two boys from fighting— in front of their father. One time, Jeff became so angry at Buster that he didn't care if they got caught, and they did.

When their father took them out in the backyard, he almost had to take the belt to Jeff to get him off Buster, who was bloodied and in need of stitches. But how could their dad explain such a gash in the emergency room? That was the last time that punishment was ever used.

Chapter Sixteen

Jeff sat on the love seat in Len Stockholm's office. On the outside, he appeared to be calm, even suave. But on the inside, he was tied in knots. He kept trying to figure out exactly what Jennifer had said to Len. He was sure she had betrayed her promise to never tell anyone.

"So, how has it been, Jeff? It's been a couple of weeks," Len said.

He's playing it cool, Jeff thought. *He's just trying to get me to lower my guard.*

"Not bad. But if everything was perfect, I wouldn't be here. Would I?"

"So, anything new to discuss since our last meeting?"

"You know."

"No, Jeff, I don't."

"I guess I've been exhibiting some erratic behavior. I've been kind of on the testy side."

"Why do you think that is?"

Oh, Jeff thought, *this guy is good. He's trying to get me to tell him everything so that I won't know he and Jennifer have been plotting.*

"Most of it is stress at work. Some of it is home stuff. Communication issues, the usual."

"What's the main stressor at work?"

"Oh, the big dogs want us to do more sales with less inventory. The typical crap."

Jeff wondered. *Was he buying this?* Len acted as if he didn't know why Jeff was here. Jeff was not going to let on about his past, but he was sure Len knew everything. Still, if Len was going to play his role, Jeff would play along.

After fifty minutes of telling Len absolutely nothing, Jeff made an appointment he did not intend to keep.

"How did it go with Len?" Jennifer asked when Jeff arrived home.

"It went well. We made some progress."

"Did you talk about any of your repressed memories? Do you want to share any of it with me?"

"Maybe later. I need some time to think about it." Jeff was sure she was on the phone with Len when he drove home. She knew everything they talked about, and what Jeff hadn't talked about—what Jeff couldn't talk about.

"You know, it's been a while. I miss the intimacy. Why don't you take a nice hot shower and, after supper, and we can have a glass of wine and talk. It's been a while since we talked."

Jeff put on his most debonair smirk, but he was panicking on the inside. He did not want to share anything with Jennifer. He was sure he still loved her, but he didn't trust her anymore. He did not know why. Had he made a mistake in telling her everything?

All through dinner, he thought about his weak condition. He did not want to succumb to Jennifer. He had to maintain the upper hand. When he went in for his shower, Jeff took an alprazolam. After the first glass of wine, he was out like a light.

Chapter Seventeen

Jeff went to Jerry's Plumbing instead of directly to the job site. There was no meeting with Raul that morning, and Jeff was anxious to see Peg. There had been a few rendezvous since their encounter at Peg's house, and they always ended in rousing, mutually satisfying sex. Jeff was very taken with Peg, but he was not sure if he loved her.

"Decided to show your face around here, huh?" Peg asked as she put her hand on the back of Jeff's neck and slowly trailed it down his back.

"Well, I just thought I'd see if I could remember how to get here," Jeff answered.

"Are we still going out tonight?" Peg asked. "Marino's?"

"Sure," Jeff said. He saw Jerry McDonald—Peg's father and his boss—come to the corner of the work van and stop when he heard the two young people talking. "I'll be there."

Jeff made his way around to the other side of the van, easing past Jerry. Peg gave him a quick peck on the cheek.

"Morning, Boss," Jeff said, focusing his attention on Jerry.

"Good morning, Murdock," he said, eyeing the boy carefully.

When Jeff got in the van, he left the door open to wait for his fellow workers. He could clearly hear the conversation between Peg and her father.

"What are you doing messing with him?" Jerry asked with a sound of urgency in his voice.

"We're just friends, but I like him. Jeff's cute. Besides, you said he's one of the best workers."

"Margaret, I know, but I meant as an employee, not as a boyfriend."

"Can't he be your employee and my boyfriend?"

"Not that boy."

"Why not? What's the matter with Jeff?" Peg was raising her voice now.

"Margaret, lower your voice. Listen, I know the family that boy comes from…."

"And they're not rich enough?" Peg was indignant. "They don't have enough money?"

"No, that's not it," Jerry said as he stepped very close to his daughter. He lowered his voice, but Jeff could still hear everything he said. "Abused kids grow up to be abusers," he said in a gruff whisper.

"What do you mean?" Jeff could hear a quiver in Peg's voice that indicated surprise.

"I know his dad. Anyone who knows his dad knows the beatings his kids got growing up."

Jeff slumped down in the van seat. He wanted to jump out and defend his father. But at the same time, he wondered if Jerry was right.

"Jeff is so sweet," she said. The quiver in her voice now indicated she was crying. "He would never hurt me."

"It's not Jeff's fault," Jerry said. "He can't help it. But that boy is going to have some baggage."

Peg turned and ran up the stairs, audibly sobbing. Jerry went around the van with a set of blueprints in his hand. He stopped when he saw Jeff.

"Oh...." Jerry started. "I guess I.... You know...."

Jeff jumped out of the van and ran to his car. He was not a plumber's helper anymore. He made enough money working for Raul. Screw this place.

Chapter Eighteen

When Jeff walked into the Big Daddy's on Commercial Boulevard in Fort Lauderdale, he had a plan. It was the same plan each time Jeff went hunting: find a bar that he did not frequent, make sure it had dancing, wear a tight shirt that showed off his physique, and go late enough that the ladies would be inebriated, and he was comparatively sober. Jeff had thus far been able to follow Raul's advice and mention his work to nobody. The time factor also made it easier since all bars close in Florida at 2 A.M. He did not want to get too wasted and not be able to enjoy his conquest.

He walked in, sat at the bar, and ordered a beer. The bar band, a cover band, was doing a rendition of a Three Dog Night song. Jeff looked across the bar, and two very attractive girls were staring back at him. The blonde whispered something in the brunette's ear, and they both giggled. As a rule, Jeff would not approach a woman if she was there with just one friend. He discovered women had this rule about not leaving another woman alone in a bar. There was that one time in Hialeah, though, where they both wanted to be with Jeff and did not mind being with each other. That was Jeff's first and only threesome, until tonight, he thought. When the song ended, a third girl, another blonde, joined them. The brunette slid a purse over to the fresh face. Within seconds, the band began playing a slow song, "Color My World" by Chicago.

Jeff drank down his beer, set the mug on the bar, and started to stand. He thought, *Might as well try to start with a slow song*. Just then, Jeff felt a feminine hand on his arm. He turned and looked into the blue eyes of a slightly inebriated, petite blonde.

"I have never done this before," she said, "but would you like to dance?"

She was as attractive as the other women and, with a little luck, she would have some self-esteem issues he could exploit. He found that many beautiful women did not see themselves as beautiful. He could usually tell right away by their response to a compliment. If he got the signal, he poured it on.

"Well," he said, "I have never been asked by such a beautiful woman."

Her response was everything Jeff could have hoped for. She was too flustered to speak as a bright red blush spread across her face. *Bingo*, he thought.

"I'm Kid," he said as he extended a friendly hand.

"Kid? What kind of name is Kid?"

"I work with a bunch of older guys. It's a nickname that just sort of stuck."

"Oh," she said. "In that case, I'm Sissy."

Jeff knew she was using a nickname just because he was. He suspected she wanted him to ask what her real name was. He never did.

"You know," she said as he led her out to the dance floor, "you have the biggest arms I have ever seen."

Jeff turned and put his hands on her hips. Sissy laid her arms on Jeff's shoulders and stroked his long, black, cascading hair.

"And I love your chest and shoulders," she said as she stroked those parts of his body. Jeff knew he had to keep making her feel special, keep making her feel beautiful.

"I work out, but not enough to get the attention of a girl like you. You're hot."

She blushed again.

After the dance, which included a fair amount of caressing each other and ended with a prolonged look into each other's eyes, they got drinks and went to a table. They talked for about twenty minutes.

"Do you want to go out and smoke a joint?" he asked.

"Sure," she said, but Jeff could tell she was a little uneasy. He learned to never push too hard and let her make the decision.

"If you're not okay with it, we don't have to," he said as earnestly as he could act. "If you don't smoke, we can hang around in here."

"No, it's not that," she said. "I'm here with some friends. I don't want to just disappear."

Jeff thought about that chick rule.

"Well, ask them if they want to join us," he suggested.

"Are you kidding?" she laughed. "I'm not going to share you. Wait right here."

Jeff watched Sissy as she walked to the other side of the bar and up to the three girls he had been eyeing earlier. They talked, they giggled, and then, they laughed. They all hugged her, and Sissy came back over to Jeff.

"Okay," she said picking up her drink. "Let's go."

"What was that about?" he asked.

"I'll tell you later," she said, taking one last sip.

They headed out to Jeff's car, his arm around her shoulder and her arm around his waist. With Jeff at a muscular six foot two and Sissy at a slender five foot three, they could have been an ad in a magazine. Jeff unlocked and opened the passenger door for her. He kissed her as she got in. Then, he went around to the driver's side to find she had slid over to the middle. She did not wait to see if he was going to light up the doobie or not, jumping on Jeff and making out.

"You're beautiful," Jeff said as he slid his hand under the woman's blouse. She grabbed his hand and put it on her bra-covered breast, still under the blouse.

"I have a confession," she finally said. "My friends," she began, "they kind of like to tease me. One of them bet me I could not get you to dance with me. I told her not only were you going to dance with me; you were going to take me home tonight."

Jeff took his hand off her.

"What's wrong?" she asked with worry in her voice.

"We're going to my motel," he answered as he started the car. She was noticeably relieved and began stroking his hair.

Jeff did in fact have a motel room in Fort Lauderdale. He avoided taking women to his apartment. He did not really want them to know where he lived.

"You have a room? Pretty confident, aren't you?"

"No. I don't live in Fort Lauderdale." Well, that was the truth.

Another of Jeff's rules involved climaxing. He believed that if the woman came first, she would cum several times, and more intensely. He would then be permitted any pleasure he desired. It usually worked. They had wild, passionate sex when they first entered the room. With the first encounter, Jeff brought her to the "Big O" orally. He then climbed on top with her legs over his shoulders. While he did not last a terribly long time, they came together. Together and naked, they then smoked that joint.

They had another session of sex, in which Sissy came two more times before Jeff finally did. The second time always took longer. Jeff then took out a small amount of cocaine he had. Sissy took Jeff in her mouth for the first time that night and aroused him again. They had another round of passion. They came together as the sun was rising.

Jeff drove Sissy home about an hour later. She invited him in for breakfast. He said he had to go to work, but promised to call her. It was not until Jeff drove off in the early morning sun when she realized he had never asked for her phone number.

Chapter Nineteen

Jeff was sure that he was safe as far as being made at El Cuervo. It took the young man a couple of weeks to heal from the fight, and there was no evidence of any stitches or anything. But just to be safe, Raul had used him sparingly the past few weeks, and not in any situation where he might be made again. It was beginning to hit Jeff in the wallet.

Jeff got to the Gire Sobre early that morning to talk to Raul. But he wasn't there. In fact, the whole team had been there for a while when Raul entered with a very agitated look on his face. Jeff knew better than to say anything.

"We have a problem," he whispered to the group crouched around the table. "In the past week, two company men working on the Crow thing have been killed in separate situations. The brass is sure there is a mole, and they suspect us."

"What are we going to do?" Bernie asked.

"Who bought the farm?" Larry asked about the two dead agents.

Raul continued as if he did not hear them.

"The agency wants us to back off 'for our own protection,'" he said mimicking concern, "but the Crow is under such pressure from the cops here and the bad boys in Colombia. We can't just walk away from this.

"This is what I'm thinking. We keep working on the Crow, and we look for the mole ourselves."

"How in the hell do we do that?" Jeff asked. "We don't know a whole lot about the Crow's operation and, at least from where I sit, we know even less about the company's operation."

"The first part is easy," Raul said. "We get somebody inside the Crow's operation. It doesn't have to be deep. But if we can get a record of who's contacting him and when, we should be able to land him."

"Kid," Raul said to Jeff, "I think you're the right guy."

"How so?" Jeff asked.

"You're the right age for the kind of guys he hires. With this long-haired hippy look, you're a shoe-in for the rebellious type. And you seem to be able to handle your pot and coke."

Jeff was shocked. He wasn't a daily user of coke, and he never went to work stoned.

"How do you…."

"On some days, you have this thing going, clenching and un-clenching your jaw. With the pot, I can smell it on your clothes when you've smoked, even the night before. Listen, kid, I've been doing this a long time. I know when someone's been around the stuff, even if they haven't touched it."

Jeff felt both cornered and ashamed.

He had always looked at himself as a good guy. The fact that he occasionally used the products that he was helping bring down had never seemed in conflict before. But it suddenly did now.

"I'm not hooked or anything," he said. "I can quit. I will quit."

"Not so fast," Raul said. "It may help us if you get in and are willing to do some stuff. It's when guys show up as cartel members, and they refuse to use that the Crow gets suspicious. If you are willing to act like one of them, it would ease some suspicion."

"Do we know who made the company guys or how?"

"No," Raul said. "All we know is if we don't stop them, more guys will die, and we'll lose the Crow."

Jeff thought for just a minute.

"Okay. I'll do it."

"Great," Raul said. "Now, as for upping the pressure on the Crow, let's start working on the cartel...."

Jeff's focus turned to what he had just gotten himself into. The jobs had always been a little dangerous. Now, he was looking for disaster. He had to be prepared, be ready—for anything.

Chapter Twenty

"When do you meet with Len again?" Jennifer asked her husband.

"I don't know. It's in my calendar."

"My guess is he told you to get a copy of the Family Jewels, right?"

"What?" Jeff asked in disbelief. "If I turn in a Freedom of Information request, they're going to wonder why I want to see them."

"But you don't even know if your name is in them. Besides, you weren't doing work for the CIA, were you?"

"Dear, I don't really know who I did work for."

Jeff took a trip in his memory.

"Kid, this is Juan Jose," Raul said. "He is a company man. He's the agent assigned to the Medien Cartel."

Juan Jose looked young and had not shaved in a couple of days, and his hair was not combed. His clothes were clean, but wrinkled and a bit disheveled. He had a toothpick in his mouth.

"How long have you been with the DEA?" Jeff asked.

"I'm not with the DEA," Juan Jose replied.

"Oh?" Jeff was surprised. "But, Raul said you were a company man."

"There's more than one agency interested in what happens in Colombia."

"CIA?" Jeff was truly surprised.

"Kid, you're asking questions again," Raul said.

"The drug trade from that country is affecting the crime rate in this country, as well as the economy and many other facets which concern our administration," Juan Jose said matter-of-factly. "Plus, one of the two guys killed recently was from our agency. We don't like thugs popping our people."

"And now, there's Bernie," Raul said.

"What happened to Bernie?" Jeff asked.

Raul had his hands in his pockets, and he was looking at Jeff in the eye. Jeff could see he was having trouble speaking. Deep in his heart, he knew why. Raul looked at his cell like they were his family, his kids. He looked down and kicked some dirt. Then, he made eye contact with Jeff again.

"They found Bernie early this morning. He was missing three fingers. Son of bitches probably cut them off, one by one, trying to get information. He had been shot in the knee cap and in the back of the head."

A cold chill ran through Jeff.

"So, what's the connection here? Are we working for the DEA working with the CIA?"

"You don't work for the DEA," Raul pointed out. "You work for me, and I work for whoever I want to work for."

"Okay…," Jeff said. "What do you want me to do, Boss?"

"*Shut up and listen,*" *Raul said.*

"*We need to get the Cubans back in charge in Miami,*" *Juan Jose said.* "*The Colombians are too brutal; too bloodthirsty. They have no concern for collateral damage. Every month, more and more innocent bystanders are killed, not to mention ever-growing extensive property damage.*

"*We are willing to give you guys some equipment and backup that we know you haven't received from our brothers in the other agency. We pay you our operative rate, and Raul gets to keep the gadgets.*"

Until now, Jeff has never had so much as a two-way radio or a listening device. When he has gone in somewhere, it was up to him if he got out or not.

"*I think I will feel safer wearing a wire.*"

"*You might,*" *Raul said,* "*if you were going to wear a wire. While we're trying to get in on the inside, the Crow's men will be really, really watching you. You'll probably get patted down on a regular basis. No wire.*"

"*We will be watching you,*" *Juan Jose said.* "*But it will have to be from a safe location. Safe for us, but safe for you, too. These are some bad people. If they suspect something, you're dead.*"

"*We have this tool,*" *Juan Jose said, holding what looked like a long microphone with a satellite dish on its handle.* "*If we aim this at you, we can hear everything said from up to 200 meters.*"

"*I need to ask you this,*" *Raul said.* "*Does your family know what you do?*"

"*No,*" *Jeff said,* "*you said not to tell anyone. They think I'm working as a plumber in new construction.*"

"*Okay,*" *Raul said, putting his hand on Jeff's shoulder.* "*After this assignment, you might want to think about telling them.*"

"You mean if I make it?"

"No, no. It's not that…," he paused, "listen…maybe…I just don't ever want to be the one who…."

"Raul," Jeff said, "shut up."

On his way home, Jeff stopped off and visited his parents.

Chapter Twenty-One

Jeff sat up in the bed. He thought he heard a noise. Jennifer was sleeping. She obviously did not hear it, but her senses were not as keen as his. All the lights were off so that "they" could not see into the house. Jeff walked around, peering out through the curtains, trying to spot them, but they were good. He could never see where they were hiding. He was sure that since he had begun trying to find a copy of the Family Jewels online, they were on to him. They probably traced his computer. He knew they could do that now. He had not made a Freedom of Information Act request to avoid raising suspicion, but he knew they had found him, anyway. He went back to the bedroom and looked at Jennifer in the bed. She had grown weary of his suspicions, but he knew they were out there. He recalled the night he met her.

Jeff's father was a plumber. Jeff had worked with him during his high school years, so his working in the field was not such a stretch. Since his dad did service work on a small scale, it was not unusual that Jeff and he would not cross paths if he worked on new construction on large jobs. Bill Murdock did not have to know Jeff had quit Jerry's Plumbing without even picking up his last check.

"I can't believe you talked me into coming with y'all tonight," Jeff said as he entered the Plumbing Contractors' Association dinner with his parents.

"Relax," Bill Murdock said. "Enjoy yourself. You'll probably meet some people you know."

"I doubt it," Jeff said. "These are the owners, bourgeoisie. I'm a working stiff, careful."

Jeff looked around. "I think I'm the only one here under fifty."

At about that time, he saw a young woman across the room who, even if he were at a dinner for models, he would have noticed. She had light-brown hair that cascaded around her face down to her shoulders, and big, dark eyes. From that moment on, he could not take his eyes off her. After dinner, he felt a soft hand on his shoulder.

"Hi," she said. "I'm Jennifer."

"Hi," he said. "Jeff."

"I was just wondering," she said, "if you were going to stare at me all night, or if you were going to ask me to dance?"

"I…I haven't been…okay, I have been…I have noticed you. But, come on, we're the only two people here who don't qualify for Social Security."

"Okay," Jennifer said. "I have noticed that. So why haven't you asked me to dance? Or at least say hello?"

"Well, first of all," Jeff said with a sly smile, "I don't know how to dance to this kind of music. And as for the hello, I am terrified at the possibility of rejection."

"Oh, I kind of doubt you experience much rejection. And as for dancing, I'll teach you." She led Jeff out to the dance floor.

"Now put your arms around me, around my waist," Jennifer said, placing Jeff's hands on the small of her back, "and I'll put my arms around you like this." She clasped her hands behind Jeff's neck. "Now, we just move to the music."

They began swaying and moving rhythmically to the mellow music. They talked. They laughed. For the first time in a long time, Jeff felt at ease. He was happy he had come to the dinner with his folks. His parents glided across the dance floor to their side.

"You had better move around," Bill Murdock said, "or you'll drill a hole in the floor."

Jeff and Jennifer had settled into talking and slowly spinning around circles, oblivious to their surroundings.

By the end of the evening, Jeff knew he had encountered a very special woman.

In the weeks to come, Jeff discovered Jennifer had a sexual appetite equal to his. He did not see himself settling down and having only one woman, at least not yet. But the more time he spent with Jennifer, the more Jeff thought that, if he ever settled down, he could settle down with Jennifer.

Chapter Twenty-Two

Jeff arrived at the Miami Avenue Bridge over the Miami River about fifteen minutes early. Raul was across the river with some backup and the listening device. It was cold, very cold for Miami. Jeff had on a sweater with his long overcoat on over it. He was also wearing leather gloves and a wool cap. He, of course, was armed to the teeth. He had his .45 at the back of his pants, his switchblade in his right rear pocket, and his MAC-10 in the pocket inside the overcoat designed just for it. The area under the bridge looked like a dump. There was a shopping cart with a few things in it nearby and a bag of garbage next to one of the bridge supports. There were bits of trash everywhere, and it smelled like a dumpster. Jeff noticed a female figure standing there as he approached. He could see her breathe in the cold night air with the sodium crime light glow beyond the shadows of the bridge.

"Did Carlos send you to clear out the bums?" she asked.

It had been almost a year, and they have never really been introduced, but Jeff recognized her right away.

"Si," he said, wanting to throw her off.

"There was one guy here when I came, but I chased him off."

Jeff panicked. It was the Latina who assisted the doctor when Jeff caught the bullet in the ass. Was she here to sell him out? She had to be the mole, the one who had been selling people out. Didn't she recognize him?

"You must be new. I'm Jenny. I help Carlos with…information."

Okay, Jeff thought, *she is the mole, and she doesn't recognize me, yet.*

But Jeff panicked. He knew he was meeting the Crow about somebody who had to be taken out, but was it him? Was she here to sell out Jeff and just didn't recognize him? Or was it somebody else she was about to have killed, another friend of Jeff's.

Jeff looked in the direction where he knew Raul would be, but he didn't see anything. He heard voices. Carlos must be here. *Damn*, he thought, *Latinos are never on time. Why tonight?* Two men passed, and they kept walking. The pretty blonde Latina had become quiet when the men passed, but she started jabbering again. Jeff could not concentrate on what she was saying. He knew his life was in great peril. He took his knife out of his back pocket and held it in his hand in his overcoat pocket.

She suddenly stepped up to Jeff and looked at his face.

"What's your name?" she asked. "Don't I know you?"

Jeff was too scared to speak. He had been made.

"You're…you're the guy," she stammered. She was inches from Jeff, standing right at the bank of the Miami River.

Jeff heard a car door slam. He clicked the knife open in his coat pocket.

"The guy with the bullet in the ass…."

For the first time since Jeff started working with Raul, he thought he was in grave danger. *I can't let this happen*, Jeff thought. But he didn't know if he meant he could not let her expose him, or he could not let himself do what he knew he had to do. He put his left arm around her and pulled her close. He could see the look of terror in her eyes. Jeff placed his mouth over hers—not as a kiss, but as a way to muffle any scream. He brought the knife out of his pocket and thrust it upwards, into her abdomen, hard up through her diaphragm. She fought Jeff ever so briefly. He twisted the knife, and blood gushed out. He felt the warmth of her lifeblood splatter on him in the cold night.

The voices were getting closer.

He backed his face away from hers. Her eyes fluttered as life left her, and she went limp. Jeff looked up. The voices were not visible yet. He let go of the knife, turned toward the river, and threw the woman into the Miami River. With slapping of the current against the barnacle-covered pilings, her splash was barely audible. Jeff quickly took off his gloves and threw them in after the mole. He looked down, and the front of his overcoat was also covered in blood. He took it off. He thought for just a second about his MAC-10 and then threw everything into the river. He kicked the bag of garbage to where he was standing to cover any blood, but he didn't even know if there was any. His knife was gone. His MAC-10 was gone. His coat and gloves were gone, and it was cold, but Jeff was oblivious. He could not believe what he had just done. Carlos and another man rounded the corner. Jeff was not out of danger, yet. He did not know if it was the terror of what might happen next or the inability to accept what he had just done, but Jeff knew he was going to be sick.

"You been waiting here long?" Carlos asked.

"No," Jeff said. "A few minutes."

"Anybody else around?"

"A couple of bums," Jeff said. He didn't know what to do, but then he thought, "and some chica who said she knew you. She went that way," Jeff added, pointing in the opposite direction from which Carlos came.

"Go get her," the Crow said, and Jeff started walking, wondering what was going to happen next and hoping that Raul had heard all and was on his way. Jeff walked out above the bridge where some cars were parked. He stuck his hands in his pocket. He knew he was either going to cry or puke. He did not know what was going to happen next.

Suddenly, Raul and Larry appeared in Raul's car, speeding up Miami Avenue. Larry was driving. They stopped, and Jeff jumped in.

As Larry sped off, Raul turned to Jeff in the backseat.

"Who the fuck was she?" Raul asked.

"Remember when I got shot at Gire Sobre that time, and you took me to the Federal Building to get patched up? The Latina who played nurse?" Jeff answered.

"The one who came on to you? I've seen her there a dozen times since then."

Again, Jeff felt wave after wave of guilt and pain.

"I had to do it," he said, now sobbing. The guilt was now replaced with anguish. "She was going to sell me out. I had to do it."

"It's okay, kid," Raul said. "She's the reason Bernie's dead. She's the reason them other two guys are dead. And she wouldn't have thought twice about having you killed."

Raul's consolation just was not working.

"I killed her," Jeff said. "I could see her dying. I was looking in her eyes as she was dying."

"But it could have been you."

Jeff decided to take it easy for a few days. But two days later, he read in the newspaper that Carlos "The Crow" Sanchez had been found, brutally murdered. It appeared that the Cartel back in Colombia thought he was too much of a liability. The charges and ongoing investigation were too much of a distraction, so they took him out themselves. He was shot twenty-two times at close range. Jeff decided to go to the Gire Sobre that day.

"I guess you saw the paper this morning," a smiling Raul said to Jeff when he walked in. "Otherwise, I did not expect you to be back this week. Did you come to join the celebration?"

They were drinking mimosas—Champagne and orange juice—and toasting the events.

"What celebration?" Jeff asked, confused.

"We found out who the mole was, and our plan with the Crow worked."

Jeff overlooked the "we" part.

"The plan worked? I thought we just wanted him in jail or out of the country?"

"Those were definitely possibilities," Raul said, "but we knew this was the likely outcome."

Again, Jeff felt ill.

"Sit down! Have some Champagne!"

"And the hooker we hung on him? How about her killer?"

"Well, kid," Raul said, putting his hand on Jeff's shoulder and speaking in his ear, "we've kind of always known that it was one of our guys."

"And we just covered it up?"

"Relax, kid. It ain't like you've never killed a woman."

That stabbed at Jeff's heart. He knew he would never be able to forget that night.

"Now, sit down and have some Champagne."

"I can't," Jeff said. "I have to go." He turned and headed toward the door.

"Hey, kid," Raul shouted. "Come back. We couldn't have done this without you!"

That was not what Jeff needed to hear. He began walking east, and then south. He had spent nearly a year of his life doing what he thought was good. It had resulted in his playing a role in the death of two people. And now that he thought about it, he wasn't so sure he had been a good guy. He knew he wasn't a good guy. The only reason he was ever "hired" was because the people in the agency were too ethical to do the crap that he had done. He came to the realization he was no better than the people from whom he was protecting our country. He was a thug.

He found himself on a bridge going over the Miami River. He looked around and saw that nobody was watching him. He took out his .45 and dropped it into the river. He was going to Jennifer's apartment. Did he love her? He did not know. Did she love him? Again, he did not know. It just seemed like the place to go.

When he arrived there, Jennifer was sobbing. Jeff was shaken, but in her current state, Jennifer did not notice.

"What's the matter?" he asked.

"My crazy younger brother told me this weekend that my mother thought I was a tramp," she started as soon as she could speak. "I went to see her today and told her what he said."

"It's true!" she yelled, returning to her hysterical state. "She thinks I'm a tramp. She knows about the times we spent the night together and when we went camping, and she knows you are not the first guy I have been with. She thinks I'm a whore."

Jeff took her in his arms and tried to console her. Reason and logic did not work. Soothing rubs and consoling kisses on her forehead did not help Jennifer.

Then, Jeff had an idea. He wanted to change his life. He suddenly realized that if her own mother saw Jennifer as a tramp, what sleazy character he would be to anyone who knew what his life was like and what he had done. It was time to change. What better way to change his life than to get married and settle down? And surely, it would show Jennifer's mother that it was true love. He rapidly thought of the elements of his plan.

He would have to stop the drugs and pot—stop or at least cutback on drinking. *One woman for the rest of his life? Sure,* Jeff thought. He could do that. Jennifer's sexual appetite should satisfy him.

"Why don't we get married?" Jeff asked Jennifer.

"What?" Jennifer asked, startled.

"Why don't we get married? I mean...," Jeff got down on one knee and took Jennifer's hand. "I mean, Jennifer, will you marry me?"

"Are you crazy?" Jennifer asked through tears of joy. "Yes. Yes, I'll marry you."

That night, they went first to Jennifer's parents' house. With the news, all the preceding day was forgotten. Jennifer's mother, who had called her a tramp hours earlier, opened a bottle of champagne and celebrated the marriage—and thereby the salvation—of her daughter.

Later that same night, the couple went to Jeff's parents' home. While they offered congratulations, Bill Murdock was considerably more reserved. He had a beer and did not offer one to Jeff.

Chapter Twenty-Three

Jeff decided he had to completely change his life. That meant getting a regular job, getting married, having kids, and settling down. Jennifer was the one who was settled. A date had been set for the wedding. Jeff had a job with a local do-it-yourself plumbing store.

Eight months later, there was a knock at Jeff's apartment door. He had been spending a lot of time at Jennifer's place, so it was just by chance that he was home.

"Raul!" It was obvious Jeff was surprised to see his old boss.

"Hello, kid."

"How…what do…how did you find me?"

"Kid, I'm not a fuller brush man."

"Yeah, but I never gave you my address. I don't have a phone. Nothing, no utilities, nothing is in my name."

"I saw the engagement announcement in the newspaper. I was able to find you through her information."

Jeff was worried now. Had he put Jennifer at risk?

"Have you told her anything?"

"No," Jeff said. "Absolutely nothing."

"You know, you just kind of disappeared. I was wondering, what happened?"

"I...I...."

"Can I come inside?"

"No. No, let's talk out here."

"Kid, I am not here to do you any harm. I just want to talk."

Jeff finally stepped back and let Raul enter the apartment. He closed the door behind him.

"Listen, kid, you know, there is a debriefing procedure you should go through."

"Raul, I can't."

"It's important."

"You know, it has been almost a year."

"Nine months," Raul corrected him.

"Listen," Jeff was desperate. He did not know what Raul wanted. He was, once again, afraid for his life. "I haven't said anything. I never will. Not to my fiancé, not to my parents...no one."

"Relax, kid," he said. "If I was going to do anything, I should have done it months ago. Everybody has forgotten about you. If I do anything now, it would make things hard on me."

"Then, what do you want?"

"I don't know. To say congratulations. To see if you want back in." Raul was the uncomfortable one now. "I just wanted to see how you are." Again, Jeff was one of Raul's kids.

"Listen," Jeff said. He was unable to look Raul in the eye. "I have done a lot of thinking, a lot of praying."

"Praying for what?"

A tear was forming in Jeff's eye. It was all he could do to maintain composure. He had a torrent of memories that just seemed overwhelming.

"Praying for forgiveness," Jeff answered.

"Listen, kid, you did what you had to do. It's part of the job."

"Well, I guess I just can't do the job."

The two men stood staring at each other without speaking. Finally, Jeff broke the silence.

"Now what?"

Raul sighed. He shook his head.

"Don't give me a reason to come looking for you," Raul said with a stern look on his face. "Have a good life." He walked away and never looked back. Jeff never saw Raul again.

Chapter Twenty-Five

The emptiness Jeff felt since Jennifer left was overwhelming, but he could not stop to worry about it. He had to get his protection made. Jeff had not slept in two days, and he had not gone to work since Jennifer left him four days ago. The phone rang a few times a day, but Jeff would not answer it, and he turned off the answering machine. He knew "they" had probably gotten to Roger, and that was the only reason he was calling. He got tired of listening to the messages on the machine.

Jeff took his 4-10 shotgun and cut both the barrel and the stock to make them short enough to fit in the small space he was creating. He drilled a hole through the remaining stock which matched the holes he drilled in two blocks of wood. The front stoop to his house—the house which Jennifer abandoned him in—was small, about four feet by five feet. Jeff also cut a piece of quarter-inch plywood the fit that space.

Jeff knew it was risky to do this in broad daylight, but also knew that if they came for him—when they came for him—it would be at night when they thought he was sleeping. So, Jeff had to rig his contraption before it got dark. He used the blocks of wood to secure the shotgun to the porch's ceiling. He drilled a hole in the ceiling of the porch to the rear of the shotgun and in the ceiling in the living room next to the door. He climbed into the attic and fished a wire through both holes. The end on the porch, he tied to the trigger of the shotgun. Jeff then tacked the plywood to cover the shotgun. He tied the other end of the cable to the inside doorknob. Jeff knew that they would most likely crash the front door. With the shortened barrel, the shotgun blast would scatter a large pattern causing much damage to many people. He could not aim it specifically, but in general, it was aimed about head height toward the front door. The blast would hit any intruder in the head and or upper back. He may not get them all, but Jeff was going to take some of them out with him.

Jeff sat on the couch, and he waited.

As darkness fell, Jeff heard a car pull into the driveway. He peered through the sheer curtains in the living room. It was Jennifer.

Oh, shit, Jeff thought to himself, *the booby trap.*

Jeff had to keep her away from the front door.

Quickly, he ran over, opened the pass-through door to the garage, and pushed the button which opened the overhead door. Jennifer paused midstride and changed her path. She entered the garage through the open door.

"I am so happy you are back," Jeff said.

"I'm not back," she said as she brushed past Jeff. "I just need to get a few things. Why is it so dark in here?"

"I...I...." Jeff was confused. He wanted Jennifer to stay. He missed her. But, at the same time, he knew she had to get the hell out, and quick, before it got dark. "Where are you staying?"

"At Karen's. But that's only temporary. I'm divorcing you, Jeff. When it's all finished, I'll be living here, and you'll be sleeping on somebody's couch."

"Jennifer, I love you."

"Married."

"How can you say that? After all these years, and you're going to let something that happened thirty years ago split us up?"

Jennifer did not know if she had ever seen or known the real Jeff. It seemed everything was a lie.

"Jeff, what happened thirty years ago, I can forgive. It's the way you are behaving now that's killing me. You don't trust me. You don't trust anybody. You're lying more and more, and you won't let anybody help you."

"I'll change. I swear. I'll go back to Len. I'll get help."

"You've said that before, and you say it now just because it's what I want to hear. But you don't mean it. It's over."

Jennifer began piling things on the sofa. Jeff sunk inside. He knew he had lost her. It was as if his whole life was coming to an end, and he didn't care if they got him now.

"Can I at least help you?" Jeff asked.

"How about putting my makeup case in the car?"

Jeff went into the bathroom and retrieved the always-ready travel bag and headed toward the garage. Before he got to the door, however, he turned and went out the front door. He thought, *Might as well put the booby trap to good use.*

Two weeks later, Jennifer requested a copy of the Family Jewels. She received it about a month later via Certified Mail ™. It was mostly a collection of receipts and invoices. The names of all the operatives had been blacked out. And there were no operations mentioned with or involving the DEA. No indication at all of Jeff's previous life.